CHASE'S

COLORING & ACTIVITY BOOK

Chase's Coloring & Activity Book
is self published by the artist and
printed by Amazon.

Imprint: Independently published

For more information on the artist
please visit: www.TiffanyDesmond.com

Did Chase enjoy his book?
Please consider leaving
a review on Amazon.

Your support helps grow my art career.
Thank you so much!

Tiffany

Dedicated to Chase

(yes, you!)

Chase

CHASE

CHASE

CHASE

CHASE

CHASE

Chase

Chase

CHASE

CHASE

CHASE

CHASE

chase

CHASE

CHASE

Chase

CHASE

Made in United States
North Haven, CT
05 December 2024

61780212R00043